Jolly's

Sacred

Songs

Timeless Journey's

By

Rev Lorraine J. Blum

ISBN 0982784309

Alchemy Publishers

Dedication

I would like to dedicate this book to my creator without whom I would never have survived.

To the angels, both here and in the spiritual Realm, for their guidance and contributions, I am grateful. Among those were my late Brothers Russell and Robert, my Mother and Father, my Aunts, Uncles, cousins and dear friends.

To Mr Woods, for his kind gift of Enlightenment and to his Grandson Prince Jorge who's faith continued to give me strength. Thank you all. To my mentor's Dr. Joseph Gilberman, ninety nine at the time of his recent passing, my son, Robert Blum, and Richard Broxton, all gentle souls, I say thank you.

Chapters

Jolly's Sacred Songs

Synopsis

Jolly, a small grey bird, healing all living creatures when he sings his sacred songs, was sent down from heaven, primarily, to watch over an unaware Angel named Rain.

An adventurous ham of a bird, Rain noticed him one day while on an exercise walk, when he was being a wise guy and whistled at her. High up on a street post he proceeded with a show of songs, finishing with a bow.

Rain could not believe what she was seeing and silently thanked God for the awesome Spiritual experience.

This is a story about relationships, their connection and importance, reminding us never to take each other for granted.

One of the three dream sequence books, it goes back through time unfolding into stories that reach out to us, bringing a profound understanding of who we are.

Preface

Believing anything is possible, I was never-
the less surprised, one day, while jogging,
when I heard a bird whistle and then go into
song. That spiritual, unexpected experience
inspired me to write this novelette of timeless
Journey's and their wondrous connection.I
only hope it encourages those that read it to
open their hearts and minds to the facts that
have surfaced in the field of Quantum
Physics proving we are all connected like
one big Hologram. Acknowledging that we
are created from a perfect spiritual design
that offers all of us infinite possibilities, limit-
ed only by our imagination, is what Jolly's
Sacred Songs hopes to encourage.

Chapter 1

The Beginning

There once was a bird named Jolly who lived in the trees of South Florida.

Rain had seen him one day on an exercise walk, and was quite surprised to hear his songs. He was actually never far away from her after that, she had thought of him as just another grey bird, until that day Though he had been told to keep a low profile, even in heaven he was always found singing his songs as though he was a Broadway star. Jolly had made many friends, among them Cookie and Chocolate, cats who now lived with Rain and her son. In fact, Cookie really loved Jolly, which was unusual for a cat whose natural instinct is to eat a bird.

Chocolate, Rain's other cat, was impressed with Jolly's singing, though he heard other birds sing before, he never heard anyone sing like Jolly. Though she remained unaware, he followed Rain all over the world. Together they went to Thailand, England, Russia, Germany, Finland, Denmark, Norway, Sweden, Jamaica, Puerto Rico, Costa Rica, St Thomas, Nassau, Paris and Amsterdam. Jolly was unique, not just because of his mission, but because he really cared and not just about angels, humans, and animals, but all of life.

When Rain was not traveling, Jolly, addicted to adventure, would grow restless. He always meant well, but he wanted to have fun. As soon as all seemed well, he would simply plan a trip, look for a place that needed his help and for a short time go to that location.

The headlines would read,

"Miracle bird flew in again, child healed."

or

"Man needed transplant and small grey bird appeared. All of a sudden human organs healed, miracles seem to take place when bird sings."

No one knew what to make of it. He was known to some as **'Super Bird.'**

However, As soon as he would appear he would disappear returning home. No one would see him again for years at a time.

Cookie and Chocolate also had a friend named Max who was a clumsy Squirrel. Jolly knew Max very well, he was present to see Max walk into a rat trap that just caught the very end of his tail. Jolly was able to help him out of it.

They soon became a circle of friends Jolly, Cookie, Chocolate and Max the Squirrel. Before long there were others, Liżard, the cross-dressing lizard that kept getting away from Cookie, who finally came to love him with his long nails and colorful personality. There was also Yanni, the musical Mouse from Greece, who stole the heart of Jolly and the others.

Unlike Liżard the lizard, Yanni the mouse was hyper-active, he had gone through a trauma losing his family and having to leave his country, alone, at an early age. This experience made it difficult for him to get close to others. He loved to hang out, but was always busy running in other directions.

Then there were roosters and several ducks. Though they did not always agree, occasionally there was even some jealousy, for the most part, they got along very well.

If there was a fight Jolly would simply sing and whatever they were fighting about they would forget forever.

Chapter 2

Macho Man

One day there was a truck of ducks, hens and roosters driving through town, while turning on a narrow road, it went out of control. Several of the animals were hurt. Jose, a rooster got loose and ran into town.

He never saw his town or family again and remained a bit angry about it. Always in a fighting mood, he was not too popular with the neighbors. He had a habit of waking them up with his screams in the early morning hours. It was not uncommon to see him being chased down the street by an elderly woman or two, with their brooms, at five or six in the morning.

You guessed it, later that day Jolly would sing and Jose's anger and sadness would disappear.

Though a pretentious Rooster, with a sort of serious nature, he was well-meaning, however, he like some of the other's, was confused. He often found himself running after the ducks.

Tuk, later his best friend, would have been a princess of a duck back home in Thailand, here she was a beauty as well. She glided down the lake as though she was born floating, the other ducks following behind her.

Though Jose loved being seen with Tuk he truly fancied Francesca from Italy, a rather thin ugly looking duck who spent much of her time swimming alone on the other side of the lake. Though he felt wonderful when she was near, he was embarrassed to show his affection toward her. This was his secret, Even though she was a Duck and he a Rooster, alone with Francesca, he would talk for hours.

He felt she understood his loneliness and pain like no one else could, as he did hers. Their conversations lasted long into the nights, but if he saw anyone coming he would quickly leave.

Sweet Francesca missed the waters of Italy, her friends and family still living there. So skinny and unattractive, the other ducks would have nothing to do with her. Here, it seemed her only friend was Jose. Although she did not have the same feelings about him as he did for her, she understood him and looked forward to their times together.

Jose wished he could feel warmth or real companionship with the more beautiful Tuk. With her Jose could laugh aloud, not caring who was around. However, when he was with Tuk, he would have to admit, he missed Francesca. Tuk simply could never fill the emptiness he felt no matter how popular and beautiful she was; though exciting, she could not understand him as Francesca did.

This was his dilemma. Appearances meant so much to him.

A winter past and the ducks came and went; Jose spent time with Tuk whenever he could. He never saw Francesca again, though there were still times he wondered where she was. He began to suffer a deep depression and stopped waking the neighborhood. Everyone wondered if one of the elderly women did not finally do him in.

However, he began to recover slowly as Jolly healed him with his sacred songs. He forgot his beloved Francesca completely. His need to look macho with the other ducks continued to take over. Soon he was back again waking everyone before sunrise. Even those that chased him with their brooms in the past were relieved to see that their Rooster was alive.

Chapter 3

Feathered Friends

Though very popular back home, having lived in the backyard of a well known bull fighter, Carlos the handsome Rooster from Spain, was now alone. Brought to town by the bull fighter's abusive manager who treated him poorly, Carlos ran away. He showed up several weeks later in the sunny city of Tenderville. He missed the Bullfighter and his family, feeling a bit lost some of the time, but loved all the living creatures around him. He later became especially fond of a duck he saw named Francesca.

Now full grown, she was popular with all the ducks.
Kind and giving, Francesca volunteered to watch over
their babies and when Carlos first spotted her she was
swimming with them.

Unaware of whom she was and how to meet her, he
found someone else, though, he never quite forgot her.
Carlos was neat and polite, unlike Jose. He could also
be loud, but he treated the females like royalty. Soon
he would be accepted by all, except, perhaps, Jose who
was always just a little stand offish when he was
around.

Chapter 4
Love at first Quack

When Carlos, the new Rooster in town first spotted Francesca, the duck from Italy, he was talking with Tuk. As beautiful as Tuk was, Francesca was like an angel to him. He thought he was hallucinating when he saw what looked like a halo of colors over her head as she went passed him. The rainbow followed her wherever she swam. Although a few ducks and their baby ducks swam beside and behind her, his eyes were glued only on her. Little did Carlos know that Francesca felt the same about him.

Tuk did not notice anything at all, she went on quacking about her day, and all that did or did not go her way, as Carlos continued to think about being with this dream of a duck floating by.

Much later that same day Francesca had come up on shore and watched as she caught Carlos sleeping on the grass.

It was evening when Carlos, waking from his nap, heard a group of ducks on the lake. He hurried to see if one of them could be Francesca. Little did he know, earlier, while he was dreaming of her, she was watching him. Many ducks went by but not Francesca. Carlos was about to give up when he saw another wave. There she was, turning the bend, swimming like an angel. Feeling a bit weak in the knees he knelt down, unable to keep his eyes off her, as she swam by.

On her way back with the smaller ones, from the side of her eyes, Francesca saw Carlos, on shore, staring, as she passed him.

"That's my man."

She quacked to herself, I will see him later.

Carlos almost fell into the water trying to see Francesca as she rounded the next bend. Weakly he got back on his feet.

 "That is my Ducky"
He screamed out loud.

Chapter 5

Winds Stirring

The supermarket seemed very crowded for a weekday, everyone was stocking up for the season ahead. Some of the shelves were empty.

While shopping for cat food and other supplies Rain and Rob ran into several of the neighbors. Later in the parking lot Robby helped Mrs. Reese who was having a hard time loading her groceries into her car. Just then Sol and his wife said hello, as they drove by, on their way out.

"Need an extra hand? They say a storm is brewing, hope you have everything you need."

Robby finished loading the last of the groceries in the car and yelled back just as Sol began to drive away.

"I'm finished. Thanks anyway."

All the neighbors liked Robby; he was always there if they needed a little help, as were they for him when he needed assistance. It was a quiet but friendly neighborhood where even the ducks, birds and cats got along.

The next year proved to be a milder one. The leaves were green and the sun was shining even brighter. Jose discovered a new Rooster had arrived in town; Popular with the ducks, Carlos was just as exciting as Jose.

Tuk had a big crush on him. Now Jose had his hands full, he actually had competition, out of all the ducks to choose from for a best friend, this Rooster had to chose his girl, Tuk.

Later that week Jose learned Carlos was stuck on a new duck named Francesca . Jose could not remember having seen her before though he seemed to remember the name. Now well rounded, Francesca had grown into a beautiful full bodied duck. He watched as all the ducks followed her.

Meeting Daisi, one of their mutual friends later that month, he asked about Francesca and her relationship with the new Rooster in town. Daisi was bigger then the others and loved to talk.

"Francesca likes charming Carlos; he seems exciting yet easy   going. She told me she was nearby watching when he gently played with the baby ducks. He is the kind of Rooster that would treat her like a doll instead of a duck."

Jose wondered why he had not seen her before and from where she had come. When he realized he had Tuk back he soon forgot, though he wondered why a part of him was not overjoyed. He put it off to never being quite satisfied, and went off to find the crowd.

Chapter 6

Life Can get Clumsy

Bumping into Max, the squirrel, as he turned the corner, he quickly noticed the blood.

"Max, did I do that?"

Max looked dazed,

"Oh no, I was walking quite fast, as usual, and went into the tree."

"I'm sorry, can I help?'

Jose asked

"Thanks no."

Max was always getting into accidents and now had a horrible bloody nose. Just then a voice rang out behind them it was Cookie,

"Not again Max? Why are you always so clumsy? You really need to work on that. Last week you almost got hit by a car, the day before yesterday you got hit by that golf cart and was lucky it just glazed you. What's up buddy?"

Almost bumping into Jose who was behind her she greeted him as well.

"Oh hi Jose, I didn't see you standing there, how are you?"

Jose looked up.

"Me? I am fine, how are you and Chocolate?"

As they greeted each other Jose and Cookie heard weeping behind them.

Max put his head down and started to cry. He remembered the time he was frozen and unable to help Cookie as she was attacked by a big monster Tom Cat. He always felt guilty about that, thank God she lived he thought, as he held his head down.

Cookie and Jose felt terrible seeing him cry.

"Max,"

Cookie continued,

"We care so much about you; we lose sleep thinking about, how, on some of those occasions, we almost lost you. We just want you to be safe. That's not something to cry about."

Jose chimed in.

"Cookie wants you to be more careful, I myself believe in democracy, you can be what you want buddy, just not sad, I want to see you happy, don't cry."

Cookie pushed Jose out of the way.

"Yeah Jose, your one to talk, he can be a happy hospital guest."

Cookie, as sweet as she always was, obviously upset now yelled again.

"Max you really have to take this seriously!"

Finally Max wiped his tears and responded.

"You guys really stayed up all night and worried about me?"

 "Max,"

Cookie replied

"We love you. You mean a great deal to us. When you hurt so do we. You need to be more careful. How long can your luck hold out?"

Max hugged Cookie. He looked into her eyes as though it was the first time he ever saw her.

"You care that much?"

Cookie gave him a big smile and repeated

"What do you think Max?"

Tired and all beat up from his experience with the tree, Max agreed he needed a change. Cookie suggested he get some rest as she and Jose left. While she knew it was not the end of Max's mishaps, she hoped some of what she said would sink in and make him less impulsive. Jose looked at Cookie.

"When did you guy's stay up all night?"

Cookie grinned

"We are always up at night; we are nocturnal animals."

Just then Yanni came dancing by, not even hesitating or stopping to talk. He yelled out with that Greek accent of his,

"I will see you guys later at the Lake, I need to hurry now."

As he passed by his radio earpiece fell off. He stopped a brief second to pick it up before he was gone from view. He always seemed in a hurry and preoccupied with his music. Though that was Max's nature as well, Max always had time for Cookie and the others.

Just then Liźard came by.

"Cookie I am glad I found you, Rain has been calling you and Chocolate for a while now."

Without a reply Cookie left to go home.

Chapter 7

Strange Curb Fellows

Jose alone now with the kind cross-dressing lizard, asked him how he came to have a friendship with Cookie, a cat of all animals. Lizard , a sensitive and good-natured lizard, unlike other lizards, would not hurt a fly. Although he had been ostracized by other animals, lizard's among them, because of his long polished nails and the way he liked to dress, he remained social and understanding. He was always easy to talk to and Jose listened closely to his sad story.

Tears fell as he spoke about his friend Liselle, the shy, lisping lizard he so missed.

"Cookie was doing her natural thing,"

He went on to explain;

"She was chasing other lizards when she caught my
friend Liselle, a sweet thing of a lizard.
Liselle, I would later learn, was not killed by Cookie,
she was tortured and killed by another cat. However, it
was Cookie who originally found her."

Bottom line was Liźard was broken hearted. After he
buried his friend he wanted to know who killed this
gentle lizard and why. Another tear went down his
check as he went on with his tale of woe.
"This was a simple lizard that was just trying to survive. She had a speech problem that others made fun
of from time to time, but she was the forgiving type,
she never worried too much about anything."

In any case, Liźard thought it was Cookie that had killed her and hunted her down for an answer. Though he realized by meeting with her and telling her all about his friend he was putting his own life in danger, he did it anyway.

Cookie never met a lizard like this and was very impressed. She explained that she was not the cat that caused his friend's death. In fact that particular cat, Checkers, died from a car accident a week later. However, Cookie admitted, she was the cat that first spotted his friend and that she was sorry she caused him so much grief. After that, she and Liźard became the best of unnatural friends.

Jose listened as Liżard told the story. It was so poignant, it reminded him of another story that was meaningful, but he could not remember the details.

All of a sudden they heard Cookie screaming and ran in that direction. The screams got louder as they got closer to the house.

Finally, they were standing outside the enclosed porch and Yanni, the mouse, was standing there frozen with Max, the squirrel. Both were horrified, watching, as Chocolate was fighting with Cookie. He was biting her and she was trying in vain to bite him back in self-defense.

"Where is Rain?" yelled Liżard.

Just then, they heard the car drive up, all of them running into the bushes, as Rain came out with the groceries. She heard the commotion as she entered the house. Screaming, she Chased Chocolate away from Cookie.

"Why did you do that to your sister? Leave Chocolate. Get out of the house right now."

She screamed.

Everyone was relieved, holding their breath, unable to help, they let out a sigh.

Cookie walked away from chocolate, limping a little, as she went.

Yanni and Max were discussing how Chocolate was treating Cookie, when Jose and Liźard approached.

Liźard was serious as he spoke and Jose, the Mexican rooster, chimed in.

"Why did Chocolate fight with Cookie like that?"
They asked,

Yanni answered.

"That is what cats do, they fight with one another."

"Rain was giving Cookie more attention than Chocolate and he became jealous."

Max chimed in and Yanni quickly added.

"When Rain went to the store Chocolate attacked Cookie. She was napping, unaware Chocolate was even there. At first Cookie would not fight back and hoped Chocolate would go away, but Chocolate refused to stop and would not leave her alone. Finally she did fight back, but Chocolate being twice her size, she really never had a chance."

Chocolate came running out of the house right up to them as they talked.

"Hi guys what are ya'll doing?"

Chocolate was one of the crowd, everyone liked him, but they did not what he just did. Liżard, as frightened of cats as he was, was first to speak.

"Chocolate with all due respect, I like you very much, but I do not like to see Cookie hurt".

Yanni,the mouse, just as frightened, spoke next.
"Chocolate we love both you and Cookie, but it both-
ers us to see any of you guys hurting."
Max and Jose were last to speak,
"Why, why did you do that to Cookie?"
They almost said it at the same time. Chocolate was
speechless; he just stared for a minute, the longest
minute for everyone around him. Then he turned
around for a second and just as fast he turned back;
"Cats always fight, that's one of the things cats do.
Cookie and I love each other, but we fight. Listen, I
have to go now, I will meet all of you at the Lake
later."

Just as though nothing happened he was off running,
then out of sight. Yanni, the musical, hyper mouse,
and Jose, the Mexican rooster, watched as he walked
away. He never looked back.

Lizard, and Max, the clumsy squirrel, still upset about Cookie, were glad he left.

Just then, Cookie came limping out and the crowd ran to her. She was calm as she spoke.

"It's ok, I am fine, Chocolate and I always fight."

Assuring everyone she would see them at the lake later, she limped back toward the house.

Later Jolly treated her with his sacred songs and Rain took her to the Veterinarian. She would have to stay home the next two days or so.

That night Chocolate felt bad and apologized for being too rough with her.

Everyone but Cookie showed up at the lake that evening, all of them singing songs under a beautiful full moon. The gang was forgiving, as usual and everyone forgot what it was they forgave.

Chapter 8
Sudden Twister

Back at the house Rain was putting medicine on Cookie's leg and Robby was watching television. Jolly was back. Outside he had travel flyers all around him, while planning his next trip abroad.

All of a sudden there was a news update; the newsman screamed and words flashed across the screen.

"There is a possible tornado about to strike right here in Tenderville."

Many of the neighbors were stocking up at the supermarket the last few days, Rain now knew why. She did have a difficult time getting the last few bottles of water on those almost empty shelves. Rushing over to the set, she put up the sound.

"Prepare for the worst."

While pointing to a hurricane map the announcer looked concerned as he spoke. The pictures on the television looked like this tornado was coming straight at them. They just looked at each other in disbelief. "How could this be happening?"

Rain yelled to Robby

"We have to go to the bathroom and fast, get some water and food."

Both went into the kitchen and grabbed what they could. When everything was in the bathroom, Robby went to get the cats. "Where is Chocolate?"

Robby screamed loudly.

Rain ran to the front of the house and called to Chocolate. She called him three times, but the sky looked ominous, about to close the door, she called one more time.

"Chocolate get home right now."
Chocolate came flying in as though he was being chased.

The winds almost tore the door off as she closed it behind him.

Cookie and Robby were sitting amongst the boxes in the bathroom with containers of food and bottles of water when Rain and Chocolate came in. Cookie looked at Chocolate, both wondering about Jolly and the others, keeping their faith all would survive, they sat closer to each other.

Rain started the prayers for everyone.

"Dear God, help all of us and our neighbors through this tornado. Bless our children, pets and all life; let our houses stand, and our community remain whole."
Just then a loud noise of glass breaking broke into Rain's prayer, the loud banging and sounds of things flying around were frightening. At one time it felt like the wall was going to gave in and everyone just held onto each other tightly.

Rain ended the prayer abruptly.
" Thank you God, Amen."

.

Chapter 9

Nature's Disaster

Outside the winds blew so hard, Jose found himself flying in the air.

Yanni and Max found cover in an open garage, but Francesca was struck by a flying piece of heavy wood as she and Carlos tried to get into an abandoned building. Liżard saw it happen and ran over to save Francesca. Although the danger from the tornado was serious Liżard and Carlos refused to leave her. Carlos shielding her from the flying debris, with his body, was then pinned under a gigantic piece of wood and glass almost as big as a house. Francesca was not making a sound, she was not moving at all.

Liżard tried to free them, screaming for help, but the winds were roaring, and there was no one in sight. Carlos screamed.

"Lizard, you are not strong or big enough to help us. Please go, save yourself."

Liżard refused to give up, pulling on the wood and glass with all his might it actually moved a little as he fell to the ground. Carlos continued begging Liżard to leave.

"Hurry, save yourself. Hurry Liżard, get out of here!" As tiny and helpless as Liżard was against the strong winds he continued to attempt the hopeless rescue. However, as he struggled to free Carlos a strong wind picked him up and swirled him away. The last thing he heard was Carlos in excruciating pain, gasping for air, but with his last breathe, repeating the words he would never forget.

"Save yourself please Liżard, before it is too late."

Just at that moment everything went black. Pulled away by the tornado Liżard spun around in the air like a piece of paper.

Although they found cover, Max and Yanni were nervous.

Yanni, frozen and shaking seemed to be in shock. Max tried to calm him down.

"It will be ok Yanni, the tornado is ending now."

Outside, just as Max looked up at the sky, Liżard came flying by and Max jumping up in the air, caught him.

Jose, now limping back, all bruised and bleeding, tried to help Max with Yanni and Liżard.

As fast as this tornado started, that was how fast it ended. They could not help but worry about the others.

Back at the house, it was silent. Rain told everyone to stay in the bathroom, as she left to check the damage. Slowly she walked through the house. No one heard anything for a while except water dripping. Even Rain's footsteps began to fade. It seemed like a long time before she finally came back.

"Ok you can come out now, but walk slowly; there is glass. Go into the back bedroom where it's safe. We will not be able to stay here tonight, and probably not for some time, so we will have to pack for us and the cats."

As he entered the foyer Robby began to see the results of the storm and the destruction it brought. Walking on something that cracked beneath his feet, neither could believe that in such a short time so much could happen. Their first thoughts were on their neighbors, they probably needed help.

Chocolate and Cookie looked at each other, what happened to their friends? If it was that bad here, how bad was it for them outside?

As Robby put Chocolate down Rain took Cookie out of his arms and put her down on the bed next to him. The glass from the window in the bedroom had not broken, probably the only room in the house not destroyed. Cookie would be safe with Chocolate there while she went outside to check on the neighbors.

They left the house immediately. Rain went in one direction, Robby went in the other. She yelled to him as they separated.

"Don't go too far. Look for a phone, ours is not working."

"Mom, I know what to do. I'll keep in touch and call you when I need you."

First she walked next door, there was no one home.

Then remembering her next door neighbor went to visit his brother who was in from New York, she spoke out loud.

"Thank you God, for saving him."

Just as she was about to cross the street she heard a scream coming from the house next to the neighbor that was away. The windows were all broken. Rain was careful going in over the glass and fallen trees.

There was a dog barking in the front room and a woman who looked like she was sleeping. Her husband was sitting nearby, his head in her lap.
"Can I help you?"
asked Rain.
The man sat still; Rain wondered if he was in shock.
"Sol can I help you?"
Sol still did not move. Rain went to get a glass of water from a silver pitcher nearby while looking for the phone.

The house was a mess, glass broken and tables over-turned; she could not find the phone. Bringing back the water she put the cup beside him. Emily, his wife, was unconscious.

Realizing she had to get help she moved fast. Just then Harry, a neighbor from around the corner came in with Robby.

"Is anyone hurt? Robby and I are going house to house. You have a great son here Rain, he's been a real help. I don't know------"

Shocked to see the condition of Emily and Sol, Harry became speechless. Rain asked them to wait as she went for help. As she crossed the street, she began to realize just how serious the tornado had been. A few of the houses were almost totally destroyed. Neighbors walking by looked like they were lost. Hoping her neighbor Sally was all right she walked faster.

The door was open when she got there, glass and wood all over the paintings Sally loved. A room so completely destroyed in just a few moments of time, she thought.

Things were in pieces all over the place, but it was silent. She could not find her neighbor anywhere. Waiting to hear Sally's cries she called out over and over.

"Sally, Sally where are you, I'm here to help you. Where are you?"
She heard nothing at all. Soon shock and denial started to set in.

Chapter 10

Life's Un-Ending Ball

Memories came in like a storm of its' own. Sally, an elderly widow had lost her husband several years before. She was always so caring about everyone. She kept the neatest house; Rain thought to herself, she is probably so sad to see it like this. Always loving their long conversations, longing to hear her friend's voice again Rain continued to search.

Coming from New Orleans, her friend would talk of the old days when she was in the 'krewe of Iris'. She described it as one of the oldest woman's club's. Sally often told her the story of how, on Mardi gras day, they drove down Canal Street on floats throwing out coins, beads and toys to all that watched them.

Then she would tell Rain about the Balls that they had every year. She could still hear her words. "All the women would wear the most beautiful costumes and gowns you ever saw. They had the beads and pearls hand sewed on those gowns, all year long, in preparation, then wore them only once. After the ball, they donated them to the thrift shops." It was an honor to join the Krewe of Iris, Sally was invited to join by one of her friends. Rain remembered Sally crying the day she told her of the secret she had kept all those years. No one in the krewe of Iris had known Sally was Jewish. Back then a Jewish person could not even be invited to attend a Ball, much less join a Krewe, so Sally never told anyone her grandmother was Jewish. She cried when she told Rain that story, feeling the guilt about hiding her heritage.

Rain understood. She too knew what prejudice could do to a person. She saw that in College from some of the teachers and felt the unfairness herself.

"Sally",

She would say.

"We all do things like that from time to time, no one is perfect, not even you."

Sally, she remembered, answered.

"Hardly me!"

Sally told her about what was called her 'Committee-man' at the Ball; a man who wore a long tuxedo with tails and white gloves who would carry a copy of her dance list. He would go to the section in the audience where the gentleman were seated and call their name before each dance. Then he would escort each invited gentleman up for the next dance, in this case, to Sally, who wore the original dance-list on her wrist.

After the dance ended the man would be escorted back to his seat and given his gift, then the next man would be called. It was the same routine for the first five dances.

All the men received the same gift, in 1977, Sally said, it was a silver goblet with the Krewe's name and date on it. That was the year her future husband was one of the men she invited to the Ball.

Memories of their conversations were like home movies. Sally was more than her stories, she was family.

Rain yelled out again.

"Sally please tell me where you are so I can help you…. Sally."

Just then she almost tripped over what seemed to be a pile of heavy laundry, she looked down and it was Sally unconscious, all wrapped in blankets bleeding.

"Sally wake up."

Rain held Sally in her arms.

"Sally please don't leave me, stay here. What would I do without you? Open your eyes."

Sally was quiet; there was no movement at all. Rain's tears fell on her friend's temple. She began to remember the loss of her own parents. Rain's parents had both been gone for a long time and Sally had been more like a parent to Rain than a friend. She began to remember more of their long endearing conversations. Suddenly Sally started to move, not too much at first, but then she began to cough. Rain was so happy she screamed

"Thank you God."

Grabbing a pillow from a nearby couch, she gently she put Sally's head on it. Realizing she needed immediate help and Promising to come right back, she ran to the phone. Falling as she went, she hit her head;

Chapter 11

The Dream

It was very dark when Rain opened her eyes, every-thing was gone, she had no idea what happened? Was she dead? She called out

"Sally"

There was no response. Totally disoriented, waiting a moment, she called again, this time forgetting she had ever been divorced; she called to her x husband.

"Jack"

Then to her son.

"Robby."

No one answered, there was just silence. It was weird, but for some strange reason, peaceful now. It was as though it was meant to be. Feeling a bit dizzy, at first, Rain got up slowly; then fell back.

When next she awoke there was some light coming in and she could see a tree outside her window. It was springtime and the branches were the beautiful colors of that season in the North. What happened to the South? She was in the South the last time she looked, how did she get to the North? What is going on, she wondered. Just then her mother came into the room. Her mother, having died years earlier, left Rain broken hearted. She could not believe what she was seeing. Not only was this her mother, but her mother was beautiful and young again, even younger than she. Her mother sat on the bed and Rain slowly began to realize she was at home, at her mother's house, in the Bronx, in the past where she grew up, but how could that be, did she go back in time? This must be a dream or death itself, she thought. Does this mean she would see the brother she had lost too, she wondered?

She did not care how this happened or was possible, only that it did and was. Now she would be able to see her family again. Having had prayed so long for this miracle, she thanked God over and over again. Her dream of telling them how much she loved them was coming true. She could hold them close again. Perhaps her guilt would lessen as well, she thought. She hugged her mom tightly.

"Lorraine, what on earth are you doing?"

After her father gave her the name Rain, her mother was the only one to ever call her Lorraine. Although she preferred Rain, how nice it sounded now. Remembering her mother being unaffectionate, back then, was not going to stop her from expressing her feelings now.

"Mom I love you"

Her mother looked at her with concern.

"Are you sick?"

Rain looked puzzled,

"No Mom, I'm fine, I just want you to know I love you."   Her mother looked at her for a long time. "Have you been doing something you shouldn't be doing?"

Rain smiled

"No ma, I really want you to know I love you, that's all".

Her mom looked puzzled.

"Ok what do you want, just tell me?"

"Ma I know I am not always as nice as I can be and I just want to say I am sorry, I love you."

Her mother laughed as she left her room yelling back she said;.

"I am not going to get you that red dress and that is that. Now get ready for school."

She screamed back as she went to the kitchen.

Memories of the red dress Rain so wanted for a School dance came flooding back. She was so upset then, it was funny now. So happy to be back in the past she reminisced, even if this was just a dream she was enjoying it.

Getting up, she went to her closet. There hanging in her closet, was a skirt she loved when she was a teenager. Plaid, bright orange and brown colors, short and tight enough then, it was hanging right there in front of her. Standing by the mirror she grabbed it off the hanger. She pulled and stretched it on up to her waist. Loving the way it looked she realized she was a size five again.

Wow, did this mean when she got to school Louie was her boyfriend too? Louie an 'A' student and an artist, her first boyfriend, was someone she loved to watch paint and draw, just like her father did.

Remembering, she had not met Louie yet and that her father died the following year, she screamed for joy. Her father must be here too.   She ran to his room and there he was, drawing a scene on a canvas.

Throwing her arms around him, she knocked it over, crying as she grabbed him closer to her.

"Rain dear, what is this about? What is my Rain bow up to now?"

Rain could not stop the tears; she missed him so,

"Daddy I love you so much"

She could not stop hugging and kissing him.

"I love you too, Baby, what are you up to? You didn't have another fight with your mom did you?"

Rain stared at her dad; she just could not get enough, even the smell of him was divine.

"No dad not anymore, don't worry, no more fights."
She hugged her father like she never wanted to let him go. He felt thin under her touch. As she held him closer, wishing she could heal him, but happy she could be with him now.

He looked into her tearing eyes
"What is wrong baby?"
Rain smiled
"It's so very ok now dad."
They talked for hours.

Wanting to stay home, she went to her brother's room first but Russell was not there, he had slept over a friend's house the night before. He was in the Boy Scouts, she later remembered, one of the Scout Leaders took them on a trip.

Reluctantly she went to school. She saw the people she had known, but at this time, back then, had not actually met.   When she said hello to Louie, her boyfriend and his sister, they just looked at her kind of strange, although some of the guys, Louie was one, seemed interested.

Trying to remember to speak only to the children she had already known at the time, every now and then, she would make a mistake. It turned out to be a strange day.

Forgetting the time difference for a minute during one of classes, she told some of her dear friends something she could not have known that freaked them out later in the day.

Chapter 12

The Parallel Past

When she finally arrived home, her brother, Russell was on his way out with a friend to play 'kick the can.' Rain grabbed him and gave him a big hug and kiss.

"I love you Russell."

He responded by screaming loudly

"Ma! Rainey is starting with me again."

Realizing she must have embarrassed him in front of his friend, she felt bad.

As much as she wanted to share these precious moments with her brother, she knew she had to let him go and hoped to be able to have some time with him later.

Her mother came over to ask what was going on and Russell yelled something incoherent as he went out the door.

"Lorraine, her mother said, Please do not bother your brother anymore."

"Ok mom"

Frustrated she could not express how much she felt in a natural way, she tried to hide her excitement; it was getting her very tired.

If only she could have done this right the first time around.

'Why is it we do not appreciate anything or anyone until we lose them,' She wondered.

The sound of the loud ringing phone disrupted her thoughts, she picked it up. Aunt Miriam, her mother's sister, one of her favorite relative's, voice was on the other end. Rain was thrilled. It was as if heaven open its door and filled the space of emptiness and pain with a visit she so needed back home.

She happily suggested they get together for lunch.

Her mother looked at her like she was crazy for even being interested in talking on the phone that long to a grown up, much less wanting to make a date with one. While she waited to take the phone she thought about it. It would not be strange if it was one of Rain's friends, but her aunt? What was going on, she wanted to know?

Rain had to assure her mother once again there was nothing to worry about.

Finally the moment arrived, Miriam was always like another mom to Rain. She could not wait to see her again. She raced into Jahn's ice cream parlor. Her Aunt was hard to miss. Even when she was older she was a beauty, but now she was incredible and all the males were looking in her direction.

She just had to follow their eyes to find her. There she was, sitting in the second booth. She went over and gave her a big hug. Surprised Miriam jumped. "Are you ok?"

Not wanting to let her aunt go and feeling the frustration of that repeated question, she reluctantly sat down across from her. They talked for over two hours and though the conversation went well and she said everything she wanted to say it was too soon for it to end. Her aunt looked at her as though she was cross eyed a couple of times and gulped her water but she continued the talk.

When the bill came Rain did not want her to leave and suggested they go shopping.

"It's getting late."
Miriam said, surprised.

Her niece seemed strange, older somehow. What had happened to her since last week, she wanted to know.

"You can tell me. Do you have a boyfriend?"

Rain laughed

"No not really, I am just happy to see you. I love you Miriam."

"You can tell me. Do you have a boyfriend?"

Rain laughed

"No not really, I am just happy to see you. I love you Miriam."

Her young beautiful aunt just stared.

"Well, I love you too. But if there was something go-ing on you would tell me, wouldn't you?"

"You know I would. I always do."

Miriam smiled, as if she thought she could wait, in case Rain was not ready to tell her.

"Ok then, we better head out; your mother is a little concerned about you."

Rain looked up.

"I know."

Miriam paid the check and kissed Rain on the cheek.

"Be a good girl; don't give your mother a hard time. I will visit sometime this week with Leslie and Carole, maybe Bernie will come too."

The experience of seeing her aunt was exhilarating she wondered if she would ever see her again. Not wanting to say goodbye, she hugged her one last time and held her tight. Her Aunt's look of concern as she left was a bit daunting.   Rain was thrilled to think she might see her aunt again with her cousins and favorite Uncle Bernie later that week.

When Rain arrived home her brother was doing his homework, entering his room she asked.

"Can I help you with that stuff?"

"Are you losing your mind?"

"I am, but I would really like to help, let's just say I am bored."

Russell needed her, his dyslexia, undiagnosed then, left him falling behind in that particular class. He had some work to make up.

As much as he would have preferred not to have his big sister near him, he needed her help. He finally agreed.

"Ok, but no funny business or I'll tell mom."

Rain was so happy to have the opportunity.

"Ok no funny business. Let's get started."

They spent the rest of that wonderful day doing Russell's homework, her loving every moment. The next day she heard her mom calling her.

"Lorraine, hurry you will be late for school."

Hurrying to get dressed, she went right to the kitchen hoping to see her father and mother before going to school. When she got there her mother was very surprised.

"What are you doing here so soon?"

In the past Rain had always been late to the table, if she ate at all.

"Mom, where is dad?"

"Your dad left early, he will be back at six, why?"

Trying to hide her disappointment, she answered.

"Oh nothing"

Her mother looked nervous, having been on the phone with her sister Miriam the night before.

"If there is something wrong you can tell me."

"No mom, really I am fine, really, I'll see you after school. I'll wait for Russell."

Just then her brother came out to have some breakfast and saw her ready. A look of shock came over his face as he sat down at the table to eat his cereal.

She sat back down and drank her milk, ate her toast and stared at her brother with a smile on her face. Her mother obviously getting more and more worried became teary eyed. She was meeting her sister later that day and together they planned on going to the school to surprise Rain.

Thrilled to go to school again, Rain hurried to finish her breakfast. Disappointed she missed her dad, she knew she would see him later, and looked forward to it. It was time to go. Russell took his books as they got up to leave.

"Bye mom"

Just as they got near the end of the walkway "Lorraine"

Her mom called

"Didn't you forget something?"

Rain looked back; her mom was holding her books in her hands with a bag of lunch.

Laughing as she ran, she was still in awe.

"I guess I must have forgotten".

Her mom looked like she was about to cry as Rain kissed her.

"You worry too much ma, see ya later."

She whispered.

The first person she saw when she went into the school was Louie, her heart almost burst. It was like being a teenager again. He did not even notice her. Then he turned back as if to give her a second look and asked her a question. She could not hear him because the bell rang just as he spoke.

Russell was saying something when the bell stopped ringing and that was not something she would ever miss again, so she turned her attention to her brother. When she turned back to Louie, he was gone. Although it was somewhat disappointing, at the same time, it was wonderful. Because in the real past, Russell would have been all, but totally ignored, as little brothers tend to be, taken for granted until we do not have them anymore. This time Russell came first as he should have back then.

Later, in the cafeteria, finished with his lunch, Louie came over to her table and sat next to Rain.

"Hi, do you live near the School?"

Rain had to control herself from laughing, having loved Louie half of her life.

That experience actually colored the way she felt about love and life, and here she was sitting beside him. Trying, as shy as he was, to meet her, he moved closer. Just then two beautiful women walked into the lunchroom and all the male eyes turned and stared as they walked over to Rain and Louie. It was Rain's mom and Aunt Miriam and poor Louie did not know what he was in for. Here he was innocently just trying to ask a girl out, probably the first time in his young life, and two woman were about to give him a hard time about it, thinking it had something to do with their niece, or daughter's strange behavior. Her mom tried to be cool as she began the conversation.

"Lorraine, why don't you introduce us to your friend?"

"Ok mom, Miriam, this is Louie Ramos, Louie, this is my mom and Aunt."

Louie looked shocked; He stared at Rain

"How did you know my name?"

Aunt Miriam laughed.

"Very funny! Aren't you a bit young to be a comedian? We made this trip to see what was happening; we can help if you let us."

Louie spoke first

"What are you talking about?"

Rain answered, "

Louie, my relatives are very concerned about me. Because I love them so much I have become too affectionate, but that is all it is, they just do not believe me."

Rain looked at her mom as she spoke.

"Mom, Aunt Miriam, I just met Louie, I already like him very much. I have a feeling we are going to be good friends, but I am fine and he has nothing to do with any of this. I just love you guys a lot and I am showing it. That is all it is. See you at home; I have to get back to class."

She kissed her aunt, and mom goodbye as the bell rang. Leaving Louie in shock, she went back to class.

The day turned out to be marvelous in spite of the confusion. Seeing her friends from the past, including Louie's sister, was a trip. Though they did not remember knowing her, it was exciting anyway. Louie did remain somewhat confused the entire day.

When school was over Rain waited outside for her brother and rushed home with him. It would only be a few minutes before she would also see her parents and later her Aunt was coming over with her Cousins and

Uncle Bernie who might be bringing his children as well. Larry and Carol were the sweetest kids she knew, proud to be their cousin, she looked forward to all of it. This night was going to be a good one. Certainly not one she would miss. She was almost home when Louie drove by on his bike.   "Hi Rain, how are you? I missed you after school, I saw you walking. Is this your brother?"

Happy to see Louie again, she replied,

"Yes it is. This is Russell."

"Hi."

Louie smiled

Russell looked bored as he put his hand over his temple to block the sun. He answered reluctantly

"Hi."

Louie looked serious.

"What was that all about with your aunt and mom today? Tell me who told you my name?"

Hoping not to confuse him any further she answered. "My mom feels I have been acting strange lately and your name is a long story."
Rain replied.

Louie looked even more confused than he did at school. "Is there something wrong, did something happen to you?" Rain looked at Louie in awe.

"Not really."
Enjoying the conversation, and not wanting to leave Louie, she was almost sorry she had to get home or seem rude, but she really wanted to be with her family. In real time Louie was still alive, her family she would never see again.

"Louie I would love to stay and talk to you but I really have to get home."

Somewhat disappointed he repeated,

"But honestly, how did you know my full name?"

Looking at Louie she wished she could tell him everything, he once meant so much to her, she did not know what to say. "Louie lets just say I met you before and leave it at that till we see each other again."

Looking puzzled Louie answered in a low unsure voice "What, when, when can we talk about this?

"Soon.

"You are not like anyone I know; I'll see you tomorrow. Turning to her brother he waved goodbye.

"Bye Russell."

Russell shrugged goodbye.

When she arrived home, her mother explained her dad
was sleeping and that she needed to be quiet.
"He took off early because Aunt Miriam was coming
over." Then she added
"He was so tired he fell asleep."

 Later that evening her Aunt and Uncle came over with
her cousins and everyone had dinner. It was a kick
seeing everyone so young again, her handsome kind
Uncle shined. She remembered their long and caring
supportive conversations. Being with her father was
everything. He showed his new paintings, they had
some real quality time together and she was able to tell
him all the things she wanted to tell him. It was a true
dream, it could not have been better.   That night she
went to bed thanking god for a most wonderful day.

If all of us were able to go back and tell our loved ones the things we wanted them to hear, she thought to herself, what a miracle it would be, but an even better one would be if no one were ever taken for granted and there were no words left unsaid.

Chapter 13

Through time

The sounds of sirens woke her up out of a deep sleep. It appeared as though she was in a vehicle of sorts that someone was driving. All of a sudden it was all black, she saw nothing, but heard

"D.O.A."

Then there was darkness.

Was she dreaming?

Blackness engulfed her again, this time waking to a couple on the dance floor. It was cloudy, she could hardly see. Was this a dream too?

A beautiful young girl with long blond curls wearing a light blue dress, more gorgeous then any gown in any wedding she ever attended was dancing by.

There were beads and pearls all over the dress and it looked outrageously expensive. The room was dim, she could hardly see, but she knew it was a big Ball and everyone there was dressed in their best. She watched as a handsome man approached the beautiful young girl; even from far away you could see the love in his eyes. He took her hand, and led her out to the dance floor in the middle of the audience. All could see this was the man, she loved and it was mutual. They were playing the wedding song. The two danced or seemed to float to the waltz, as though they had danced to this song many times before. After the dance he stopped and took a rose from the inside of his jacket and gave it to her.

Just as she accepted it, he was escorted back to his seat by another man in a full dress tuxedo, wearing white gloves. The beautiful young girl watched as he walked off the dance floor. The new song started, now dancing with someone new, she counted the minutes until she could see him again.

As he returned to his seat he was given a gift. He tore open the beautiful silver wrapping and pulled apart the paper inside to find a silver goblet. He read the words inscribed on it.

"Krewe of Iris 1977."

What a strange dream, thought Rain, beyond time itself. She wished there had been this kind of love and affection in her previous marriage. The sounds were getting louder, one voice sounded like Robby's, but it was getting dark again and it faded to nothing at all.

Chapter 14
Back at the Ranch

Chocolate and Cookie were talking with Max, and Lizard when Robby came home. All but Chocolate hid under the bed when he walked in. First he went through the drawers, then into the bathroom and into the kitchen. He was taking things out of the cabinets and refrigerator adding them to the already packed bags.

Cookie told Lizard and Max they probably would be moving out for a short time, to please tell the others they will not be seeing them for a while. Max began telling them what happened, outside, during the wild tornado.

"Apparently Carlos and Francesca got hurt in the Tornado and everyone is concerned."

The rumor was a tree fell on the Duck, and parts of a house hit the Rooster. They heard that, except for a cut here and a bruise there, everyone else was fine
"All the others managed to help each other find shelter."

Liżard said.
Although their happy abodes were in disarray and they would probably never be the same, most of them were alive, now praying for Francesca and Carlos. Jolly was probably singing his sacred songs to them now.

Back in the room now packing another bag, holding back the tears, Robby tried to speak with complete control.

"Chocolate, Cookie, we are leaving. Mom is sick in the hospital and we need to move out."

Trying to keep calm, he continued packing.
Cookie looked at Chocolate, they had not known Rain
was hurt, they wondered how bad it could be. Lizard
and Max heard and quietly went out the way they
came in through the broken side window.

They had to find Jolly as fast as they could. He would
heal Rain, they thought.

Joe, a neighbor, waited as Robby put the cats and bags
in the car. Chocolate and Cookie were frightened, they
hated to leave, but they knew there was nothing else
they could do. It was a mess anyway, and as soon as
things were cleaned up they would probably return.
Getting into the car was scary; they wished their
friends could come.

Joe drove slowly; Robby looked out of the car
window as they drove down the street. Trees were
down and cable was everywhere, Joe was careful as he
left the neighborhood.

It was fortunate they were able to lease his condo for the season otherwise they would have had to get a hotel. Robby's thoughts continued. The place was large and there was plenty room for the cats. Since it was on the ground floor they could go out. It had a nice patio. Robby tried to think of anything other then Rain, but everyone, including him, remained worried.

Finally in the Condo, Cookie and Chocolate stood by the phone listening as Robby called the hospital. He did not say a word for a long time, finally he said "Alright I will come right over." He closed the main light and went right out, locking the door behind him. Chocolate looked at Cookie and Cookie just started to cry. Chocolate sat closer to her and put his paw on her cheek. Robby ran into the hospital over to the nurse's station,

"I am Robby, Rain Bach's son."

"Rain Bach, Rain B-a---c--h, let me see. Oh yes"

said the Nurse

"The Doctor would like to see you. By the way is that grey bird yours? Wait here a moment."

Robby waited what seemed to be an hour, but he looked at the clock and only five minutes had gone by. What did that nurse mean about the bird he wondered, is this a Mental Ward? A man in a white jacket approached him.

Robby was surprised the Doctor was so young. He looked like he was just a little older than Robby's camp counselor.

Dr James sat down next to Robby. As kind as he could, he told Robby he was sad to have to tell him that his mom's friend, and his neighbor from across the street, Sally Reese, had passed away. He went on to explain he had not yet told this to his mom.

"Your mom is in shock after a severe blow to the head due to a fall. Though she has been in and out of consciousness, she has been in shock for some time, it was not appropriate at that time to tell her about her friend. However, she is recovering nicely and starting to come out of shock."

The doctor felt if Robby knew, before his mom did, it would easier. Although he was so young, Robby seemed to understand.,
"I do understand."
The Doctor believing that statement to be true continued.

"Your mother has been unconscious for a while now, don't worry if she seems to forget things easily or becomes confused, she will probably fall asleep at times too. It will take a while until she's the way you remember her. Do you want to ask me anything?"

Fidgeting and anxious to see his mother Robby looked up at the doctor.

"No. That's ok. Can I see her now?"

Though confused himself, and saddened by Mrs. Reese's death, he was so happy his mom was ok.

Entering her room, he saw her in a sound sleep. "Wow!"

He thought out loud, his voice in a mild pitch "She looks like an angel."

She remained still, her eyes closed. He sat in the chair nearby, in the dim lit room and waited.

The sun coming into the room in the early morning woke him up. Just as he was about to close the curtains she opened her eyes. At first, she did not recognize him calling out loudly.

"Russell is that you?"

Robby was so happy he almost tripped,

"No mom it's me Robby!"

Confused she questioned.

"Robby? Where are we? What happened? Why am I here?" Robby held her hand.

"Mom, wait, I will let the Doctor explain."

Ringing the bell he now had in his hands since she woke up brought the Nurse in with a needle. Rain stared with disbelief at the needle.

"Oh no not me, I want to talk to a Doctor first."

Before her last word, was out of her mouth, in walked Dr James. "Ms Bach I see you are awake, welcome back to the living, how are you feeling?"

"Not like having a needle, unless it is necessary."

The Doctor laughed

"Fair enough, let's have a look."

Examining her head, he asked everyone to wait outside.

"How do you feel, do you know who I am?"

She adjusted her eyesight. Yes I see.

"The Doctor, I presume."

"You must have had some dream; you did a great deal of talking while you slept the last day or two."

He removed the entire bandage and examined her head further. "You have quite a bump but it is healing nicely."

Then he sat down and gently told her about her friend Sally, whose funeral she missed.

"Would you like to reconsider having a shot to calm you down?"

Rain looked sad but refused.

"I just want to say a prayer for my friend."

The Doctor left the room, asking those outside not to go in for a few minutes.

Rain knew Sally was with her love, that even time and death could not keep them apart.

She now understood the dream she had of the girl with the blond curls and the handsome man who swept her off her feet, at the Ball in New Orleans, back through time. Although she would miss her friend, she knew Sally and her husband were finally together at home, in peace. She whispered her final goodbye.

Chapter 15
It's Never Over.

Jolly was very busy he had his work cut out for him and just when he planned a great get away. He could not save everyone, Not Sally and no, he was not able to save Carlos and Francesca, but he saved hundreds of others including Rain and Emily. Li zard and Max, a very unlikely pair of loving friends, build a tree home together.

Yanni, as hyper as ever, became even more interested in learning music and became closer to the Rat from Russia who was a distant cousin to the Rat from Amsterdam. Together they owned a violin of which they used to teach Yanni key notes, all sharing an attic together.

Jose still cares for Tuk, but feels like there is something missing.

Chocolate and Cookie miss their friends and look forward to the day they will all be together again.

Jolly is always around ever looking out for Rain if she should ever need his singing. After all, he is a ham, a Broadway star.

Who can belt those songs out like he can?

His bags however are always packed in case there is an exciting trip ahead for an exceptional bird who's incredible talents can be heard…………..

Any agents in the audience for a bird like Jolly?

Rev. Lorraine J. Blum _revrain@revrain.com_

Rev BlumWould love to hear from you. You can reach her at her E-mail or number. Peace be with you always.

561-866-9041 or 561-927-0384 and

Lorraine@lorraineblum.com

Chocolate With His Top Hat & Tie
& Cookie came Home can be purchased at Alchemy Publishers.com

www.ingramcontent.com/pod-product-compliance
Lightning Source LLC
Chambersburg PA
CBHW072231190626
46809CB00017B/1840